Dealing With...

STEPFAMILY

by Jane Lacey
Illustrated by Venitia Dean

PowerKiDS
press

Published in 2019 by **The Rosen Publishing Group, Inc.**
29 East 21st Street, New York, NY 10010

Cataloging-in-Publication Data
Names: Lacey, Jane. | Dean, Venitia, illustrator.
Title: Stepfamily / Jane Lacey; illustrated by Venitia Dean.
Description: New York : PowerKids Press, 2019. | Series: Dealing with... | Includes glossary and index.
Identifiers: LCCN ISBN 9781538339114 (pbk.) | ISBN 9781538339107 (library bound) | ISBN 9781538339121 (6 pack)
Subjects: LCSH: Stepfamilies--Juvenile literature.
Classification: LCC HQ759.92 L33 2019 | DDC 306.874'7--dc23

Editor: Sarah Peutrill
Series Design: Collaborate

Manufactured in the United States of America

CPSIA Compliance Information: Batch #CS18PK: For Further Information contact Rosen Publishing, New York, New York at 1-800-237-9932.

Contents

WHAT IS A STEPFAMILY?

If your mom or dad is living with a new partner or has married again, they make a new family called a stepfamily.

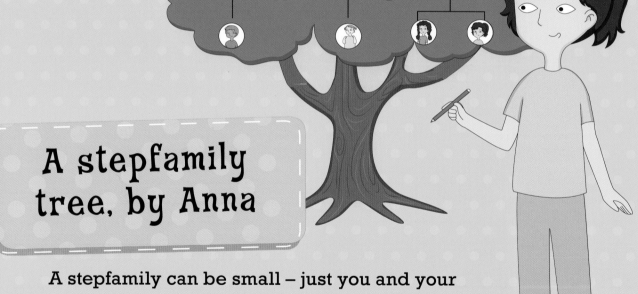

A stepfamily tree, by Anna

A stepfamily can be small – just you and your mom or dad plus your stepmom or dad. It can be big, with lots of stepsisters and brothers.

You might have two moms – your own mom and your stepmom. You might have two dads, like Anna – your own dad and your stepdad.

Caden's mom, Helen

My stepdad, Don

Mom

Dad

My stepbrother, Caden

My half-sister, Carrie

My sister, Lily

Me

Anna's story

I am part of a stepfamily. When Mom and Dad got divorced, my sister Lily and I stayed with our mom. Then Mom got married again. Her new husband, Don, is our stepdad. Don's son Caden came to live with us. He's our stepbrother. So our mom is Caden's stepmom! Carrie is Mom and Don's little girl. We all think she is really sweet!

EVERYTHING'S CHANGING!

Jacob and his dad have been on their own for a long time. Now his dad's partner, Gilly, and her two kids are moving in. Jacob doesn't want things to change.

Jacob's story

Dad and I are happy together. I like the way we do things. I don't mind seeing Gilly and her kids sometimes, but I don't want them living here all the time. I don't see why things have to change.

What can Jacob do?

He can:

* talk to his dad and say he is worried about Gilly and the kids being there all the time
* ask if he and his dad will still have time together

What Jacob did

I told Dad I like it when it's just him and me at home. I don't want things to change. Dad said he loves me, and he loves Gilly, too. He wants to be with me and with her.

He promises we will still have time together — just him and me. I think I'll get used to sharing Dad.

MY STEPDAD'S NOT MY REAL DAD

Daniel's mom has married again, and Daniel is having trouble accepting his new stepdad. He loves his own dad. He doesn't want another dad.

Will

Will is Daniel's friend

My mom and dad like having my friend Daniel around. He's always nice and polite to them. He even cleans his plate after dinner! But he's different at his home. He's really rude to his stepdad.

Daniel's story

Geoff is only my stepdad. He's not my real dad, but Geoff wants me to call him "Dad." Well, I won't! The only person I'll ever call "Dad" is my real dad.

Geoff thinks he can boss me around and tell me what to do! I hope that if I'm disobedient and rude to him, he'll get fed up and go away. I'm afraid if I'm nice to him, he might stay. So I'm not nice to him, and I don't call him anything.

Geoff

Daniel

What can Daniel do?

He can:
* talk to his mom about how he feels about Geoff
* ask if he can call Geoff by his name instead of "Dad"
* start to be polite to Geoff and treat him with respect

What Daniel did

I talked to Geoff about what I should call him. I said I would rather call him "Geoff" instead of "Dad." Geoff says he doesn't mind! Now he understands why I didn't want to listen to him before. Geoff and I get along much better now.

A stepdad's story

I love Ben and Sam's mom. I love Ben and Sam, too.
I want us all to be a happy family.

Ben and Sam love their dad very much. They were
afraid I wanted to take their dad's place. They didn't
want to like me.

I explained that I don't want them to stop loving
their dad. I just hope they can like me, too. That
made them feel a lot better. We are getting used to
our new stepfamily. It's getting better all the time.

WILL MY STEPMOM STAY WITH US?

Riley's dad has a new partner, Jane. He says Jane is going to be Riley's new stepmother. But Riley is worried that Jane won't stay with them for long.

Emma

Riley

Riley's story

My dad's ex-partner Emma lived with us for a long time. She was my stepmom, and I really liked her. I was sad when she and Dad broke up. Now I'm worried my new stepmom will leave us, too. I'm starting to like her a lot already.

What can Riley do?

She can:

★ tell her dad she is afraid her new stepmom will leave

★ ask how she can be sure Jane will stay and explain she felt sad when Emma left

★ say she doesn't want to feel sad like that again

What Riley did

I told Dad how sad I was when Emma left. I cried and cried. I said, "How do I know Jane won't leave, too?"

But Dad said, "Jane and I are getting married." I'm going to be a bridesmaid! Now I know they both really want to stay together forever.

13

I FEEL LEFT OUT

Elliot is an only child. Now he has a new stepbrother and stepsister who play together all the time. This makes him feel left out.

Tom

Tom is Elliot's friend

I'm an only child, the same as my friend Elliot. It can be lonely at home sometimes. I wish I had a new stepbrother and stepsister like Elliot. But he said he feels lonelier than before!

Elliot

Elliot's story

My stepbrother and stepsister are used to playing together. They have lots of fun, but they don't ask me to join in their games. They whisper and have secrets with each other.

I think my mom spoils them. She doesn't make them eat their vegetables and she even cleans their bedroom for them! I have to eat all my vegetables and clean my own room. I think Mom loves them more than she loves me. I feel left out.

What can Elliot do?

He can talk to his mom:

★ tell her that he feels that she loves his stepbrother and stepsister more than him
★ tell her she seems to have fewer rules for them than for him
★ explain he feels lonely and left out

What Elliot did

I told Mom how I felt. She said she would try harder to be fair. Mom plays cards and games with us all, and we have fun together. Sometimes I play with my stepbrother and stepsister without Mom now. Most days, Mom makes sure we spend time together — just Mom and me. I don't feel left out anymore.

A mom's story

When I got married again, my daughter Amy had a new stepdad and two stepsisters. I thought it would nice for her to have someone to play with. But Amy's stepsisters played together, and Amy said she felt left out. Her stepsisters said Amy wouldn't join in their games. So I've started taking them all swimming, and they have a great time. Now that they know how much fun they can have together, they are playing together at home, too. Amy and I still have fun together when my stepdaughters visit their mom.

WHY DO I HAVE TO SHARE?

Tilly is used to having a bedroom of her own. Now she has to share her bedroom with her stepsister. But she doesn't want to share it.

Kerry

Eve

Tilly

Eve is Tilly's friend

When I go to play with my friend Tilly, we always play in her bedroom. But now her stepsister Kerry is often there, too. Tilly's room is so full with Kerry's bed and all Kerry's stuff, there's hardly any room for us!

Tilly's story

I used to have my room all to myself. Now I
have to share it with my stepsister, Kerry.
She's older than me. She likes different
things. There isn't really enough room for both
of us.

When Eve comes over, Kerry's always there.
So now Eve and I play downstairs. But when
Kerry has her friends over, I still have to go
downstairs! It's not fair!

Kerry wants a room of her own and so do I,
but there isn't another bedroom in our house.

What can Tilly do?

She can:

★ decide with her stepsister the times they can have the room to themselves
★ make their own private spaces in the room
★ remember it's hard for her stepsister to have to share, too

What Tilly did

Kerry and I agreed that whoever has a friend over gets the bedroom. I also have the bedroom to myself when I get home from school. Kerry hangs out with her friends after school. We aren't very tidy, but we keep our things on our own sides of the room. Sometimes we like being there together now.

Liam's story

When Mom and I moved into Mom's partner's house, I had to share a room with his son, Bobby. Bobby's younger than me, so we go to bed at different times. If I read with the light on, it wakes Bobby up! Then he gets up early and wakes me up! So we hung up a curtain between our beds. If Bobby calls through the curtain, I don't mind. Sometimes I tell him stories if he can't get to sleep.

MY STEPMOM'S RULES AREN'T FAIR!

Leo doesn't like his stepmom's new rules. He thinks her rules are too strict and that they aren't fair. He argues with her all the time.

Harry

Harry is Leo's friend

My friend Leo thinks his stepmom is too strict. I don't think she is really. She only makes the same rules as my mom, like helping with the dishes. Leo sticks to my mom's rules without complaining when he's at my house.

Leo

Leo's story

My stepmom treats me like a little kid. My stepbrothers are older than me, and she sends me to bed earlier than them. She doesn't let me watch the TV shows I want, but she lets them watch what they like! When I go to stay with my mom, she lets me stay up late, and we watch TV together. We eat chocolate, too. But my stepmom never lets me have chocolate! I argue with my stepmom and say, "It's not fair! My mom lets me! You can ask my dad."

What can Leo do?

He can talk to his dad and stepmom together:

★ say why he thinks the rules aren't fair
★ talk about what his mom lets him do
★ see if they can all agree on some rules
★ when he has agreed to the rules, try to stick to them without arguing

What Leo did

I talked to Dad and my stepmom about things like my bedtime, cleaning up, and watching TV. Now that Dad and I have agreed on rules with my stepmom, I stick to them — most of the time! When I'm with my mom, she spoils me a bit. But that's OK because she doesn't get to see me all the time.

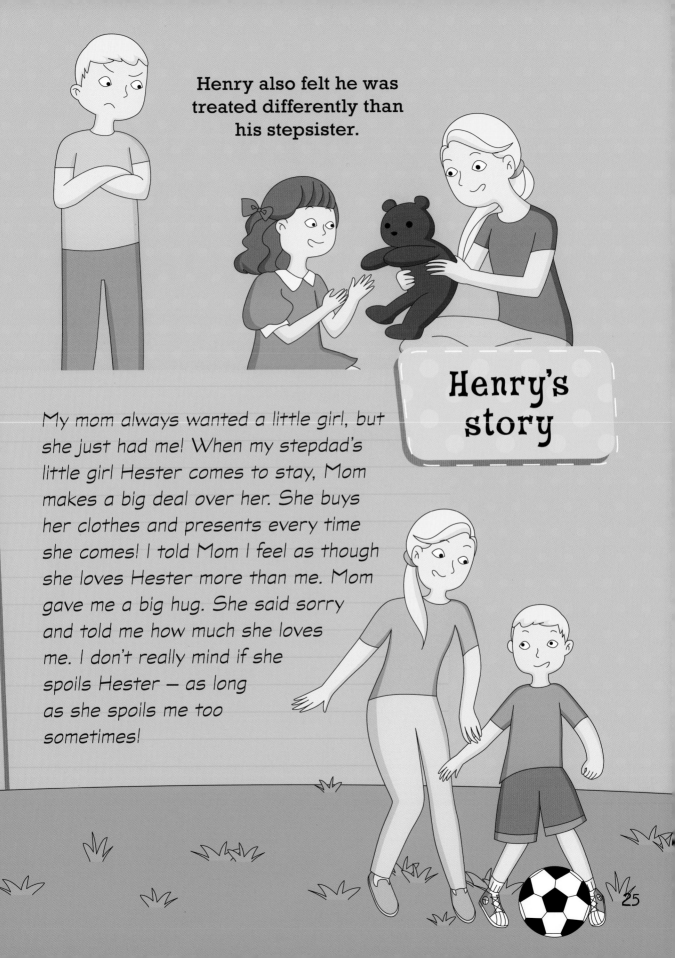

Henry also felt he was treated differently than his stepsister.

Henry's story

My mom always wanted a little girl, but she just had me! When my stepdad's little girl Hester comes to stay, Mom makes a big deal over her. She buys her clothes and presents every time she comes! I told Mom I feel as though she loves Hester more than me. Mom gave me a big hug. She said sorry and told me how much she loves me. I don't really mind if she spoils Hester — as long as she spoils me too sometimes!

I LIKE SPENDING TIME WITH MY STEPDAD MORE

Kyle gets along well with his stepdad. He is worried that his own dad would be unhappy if he knew.

Kyle and his stepdad

Kyle's story

I don't look forward to seeing my dad. We don't do anything anymore. He wants to know what is going on at home, but he gets upset when I tell him! I really like my stepdad. He's fun, and he makes Mom happy. I feel bad for my dad, but sometimes I think I like my stepdad better.

What can Kyle do?

He can:

★ remember it is all right to love his stepdad
★ tell his dad he doesn't want to talk about home with him
★ ask his dad if they can do things together when they see each other

What Kyle did

I told Dad I didn't want to talk about home. He said that was OK. I said I wanted to learn Judo on Saturdays. Dad found Judo classes near him. Now we are both learning Judo together! It's fun. We both really enjoy it.

Kyle and his dad

WE'RE GOOD FRIENDS NOW

Arran and Bonny are stepsiblings. They didn't get along with each other at first.

Arran and Bonny's story

 Arran: When I heard I was going to have a stepsister, I was disappointed. I wanted a stepbrother.

Bonny: Yeah! And I wanted a stepsister. But I got Arran!

 Arran: I thought Bonny would only like girls' stuff — dolls and makeup and pink things.

Bonny: I thought Arran would be crazy about football and have smelly socks.

 Arran: Actually, I like riding my bike more than football. Bonny's got a cool bike, too, so we ride our bikes together.

Bonny: I love reading. Arran has lots of books, and he lends me some. They are great. I lend him my books, too. It's like having a whole library at home!

Arran: When Bonny has her friends over, I give them some space. And when I have my friends over, she gives us space, too.

Bonny: But we had a joint swimming party for our birthdays. Our friends had a really good time together. So we know our friends get along well, too.

Arran: Bonny went on vacation with her mom for two weeks and I really missed her.

Bonny: I thought it would be great to have Arran out of the way when he visited his Grandma, but I missed him, too.

Arran: Bonny and I didn't think we would like each other. But now we're good friends.

GLOSSARY

Divorce
A married couple become divorced when they sign papers that mean they are not married anymore.

Fair
A rule or decision is fair when it is good for everyone involved.

Lonely
People sometimes feel lonely when they have to spend a lot of time on their own.

Married
When two people sign certain papers, they become married.

Partners
Two people who are in a romantic relationship.

Private
You are private when you choose to be alone or keep something to yourself.

Respect
You respect someone when you are polite and kind to them.

Rules
Rules are things that you must obey. For example:
★ bedtime at 8 p.m.
★ finish homework before watching TV

Share
You share when you tell or give things to other people and you don't keep things to yourself.

Stepfamily
A stepfamily is made when two people who already have kids get together to make a new family.

FURTHER INFORMATION

Books

Geisen, Cynthia. *Growing Into a Family: A Kid's Guide to Living in a Blended Family.* Abbey Press, 2013.

LeMaire, Colleen. *I Have Two Homes.* CreateSpace Independent Publishing Platform, 2014.

Lisa Cohn and Debbie Glasser Ph.D. *The Step-Tween Survival Guide: How to Deal with Life in a Stepfamily.* Free Spirit Publishing, 2008.

PowerKids Press has developed an online list of websites related to the subject of this book. This site is updated regularly. Please use this link to access the list: www.powerkidslinks.com/dw/stepfamily

INDEX